Also by Pauline Barclay

Magnolia House
Satchfield Hall
Sometimes It Happens…
Storm Clouds Gathering
In The Cold Light of Day
The Wendy House
The Birthday Card
Serendipity
Past Secrets and Lies

You can find out more about Pauline on her web site and Blog

www.paulinebarclay.co.uk
https://paulinembarclay.blogspot.com

Tormentors

Pauline Barclay

www.paulinebarclay.co.uk

To Kim

Hugs

Pauline

x

Tormentors

Dedication

This booklet (short story) is dedicated to the amazing Samuel Ridge-Ward and his wonderful mum, Karen Fulcher.

Whilst this story is fiction, as are all of the characters, Sam and his mum lived through a very similar horrific situation with scars they will carry for the rest of their lives.

I have written this booklet to highlight just how life-threatening bullying can be. It is my hope it will help identify any hint of bullying in your family and if so, please deal with it and, if necessary, seek help before it is too late.

All royalties from the sale of this booklet will go to Red Balloon, Norwich, England.
https://www.redballoonlearner.org/

Chapter ONE – Dillan

With his head bent and his hands stuffed deep in his pockets, Dillan stood alone in the middle of the rain-soaked pavement where several puddles surrounded him. Rain dripped from his blonde curly hair and his fringe flopped over his eyes. A small cut bled at the side of his right cheek. He'd been holding his breath and right now felt as if his lungs would explode. Feeling he might faint, he let out a long exhale, then took a few gulps of air; suddenly he felt sick. Not wanting to throw up, he swallowed down a mouthful of bitter bile. He needed to get home, yet despite knowing this, he felt rooted to the spot. Glancing up at the grey leaden sky he noticed the rain had stopped. He stood motionless in the puddle and lowered his gaze. He removed his hands from his pockets and reaching down he picked up his mobile phone. He wiped off the water and it pinged at his touch. 'You still work,' he cried with relief then turning it over, he stared down at the screen and felt the prickle of tears; the screen was broken again. Through the fragments of glass and unshed tears, he saw he had fifteen unread messages on Whatsapp. Even as he took this in, his phone pinged alerting him of another message. He pushed down a sob that threatened to choke him and closed his eyes. Then snapping them open, he looked at his phone screen; it was still broken. He hadn't imagined it! He bit down on his bottom lip and at the same time ran a finger over the broken glass. His mind reeled at the events that had just taken place and wished he could slip between the broken fragments and disappear. He tried not to let the tears spill. He pushed his knuckles to his eyes to help stop the flow, but it didn't work. Knowing he must head home; he wiped the back of his hand across his face. The last thing he needed was to be seen crying. Life was bad enough.

Ignoring the number of messages and the constant pinging, Dillan pushed his phone into his jacket pocket and sighed at the knowledge he'd have to explain to his parents about the broken screen. No way could he tell them the truth, instead he would explain that it had fallen out of his pocket. Of course, he'd told that story before and thankfully, they'd given him the money to get it fixed. Somehow, he didn't think they'd believe him this time. He'd just have to think fast and come up with a plausible reason, but right now he didn't think he could think, let alone think fast!

With the need to go home, he checked around to make sure he was still alone thankfully he was. Relieved, he set off along Carlton Road. His home was halfway down. Albion House was like many of the properties in the road, having large garages and drives big enough to turn a family car around in. His parents regularly banged on to him and his older sister, Amelia, about how lucky they were to have such a beautiful home to grow up in. He had no idea where they were coming from, what he did know was that Amelia was the lucky one, she'd gone off to university. Dillan missed her beyond words and just thinking about her had tears welling in his eyes. Sniffing at his unhappiness, he didn't think he was in the slightest bit lucky; he was still here! What was a lovely home when you had no friends? His best friend, Amelia had left too. He'd give anything to swap his so called, beautiful home for a few friends or even just one.

Making no attempt to avoid the puddles, Dillan tried not to let his mind go over and over what had happened, but his head kept pressing the replay button. Would it ever stop?

Lost in his thoughts, he almost walked past Albion House. He stopped and stood at the bottom of the drive. To his disappointment. his mother's car was there. He let out a loud sob knowing that now he wouldn't be able to sneak in and go straight to his bedroom. As tough as the situation was, there was one silver lining: his father was away on business. Another project that kept him abroad for months. He missed him too. On the occasions he was home, he was stressed, tired and could be moody, but he always had time for him. Why couldn't they live in a small house and all be at home together? But he knew nothing was going to change anytime soon.

Dillan adjusted the shoulder straps on his backpack and headed to the front door. His feet crunched on the gravel drive as he mentally worked out what he was going to say about the broken phone screen. He could already hear what his mother would say. *Dillan we're not made of money, this is the third time in as many months…* He was certain his pocket money would be reduced to pay for its repair. The thought of having less money added a further problem to the list he juggled each day. He didn't want to think about that right now - the broken screen was enough. Resigned to his fate, he slipped his key into the lock and pushed open the front door.

Chapter TWO – Dillan

No sooner had Dillan shut the front door when he heard his mother call out. He groaned. He just wanted to escape to his room; now he was trapped.

'Dillan, where have you been?' Charlotte's voice echoed down the large hall, her trainers squeaking on the highly polished parquet flooring as she headed towards him. In her early forties, five foot ten inches, slim and when not at work as an accountant or looking after her family, Charlotte loved to go for a run to keep herself fit and slim.

On seeing Dillan, Charlotte came to an abrupt halt and stared at him. 'Good grief! What have you been up to? Look at the state of you!' She pointed at his face and then at his lower body. 'You have a cut on your cheek, your hair is dripping and your trousers which were new last week look ruined. As for your shoes!' she cried, her voice filled with annoyance as she took in the state of her son.

Knowing he needed to hold it all together, Dillan stared down at his shoes and trousers and realised both were covered in mud. He'd forgotten about the mud. He clenched his teeth together at his stupidity. He'd been more worried about his phone and hadn't paid attention to his clothes. Not that it would have made any difference, but at least he could have been prepared for his mother. The black trousers were part of his school uniform and his shoes were smart black leather lace ups. The school, Thorpe Manor, had a strict uniform code. He didn't want to think what the teachers would say if they saw the state of him.

Charlotte dashed to the downstairs cloakroom and rushed back clutching a wad of tissues and a hand towel. Instantly, she wiped at the cut, then before Dillan could make a move, she draped the towel over his dripping hair.

Taking the towel from his mother, Dillan quickly ran it over his hair before handing it back.

'So, what happened?' Charlotte asked, gripping the damp towel whilst fussing in an attempt to help remove Dillan's backpack. With the bag on the floor, Charlotte insisted he kick off his shoes and strip off his trousers where he stood. 'I don't want mud traipsed all over the floors and if I take them now, I can get them straight in the washing machine.' As she spoke, Charlotte continued to fuss.

'Mum!' Dillan cried, raising his hands as if to push her away, 'I'm not a baby!' He stepped back to create space between the two of them. Hearing his phone ping several times, he closed his eyes. Not more, he silently pleaded. He ignored them.

In an exasperated tone, Charlotte asked, 'Don't your friends have nothing better to do than keep messaging you?'

‘It’s the homework group,’ he lied as his phoned pinged again.

‘The sooner we get you into clean pants, the sooner you can get on with your homework.’ As if calming down, she smiled at her son. ‘I’ve made you a sandwich and a drink. Dinner will be at the usual time.’

Relieved his mother had changed the subject, to his delight, she turned and headed back to the kitchen. Feeling the need to see how many messages he had, he pulled out his phone. His mother suddenly turned and stared at his hand.

'Dillan what’s happened to your phone?’ she asked, glaring at the broken screen as she stepped back towards him.

He so wanted to scream at being such an idiot and not leaving his phone in his pocket. He’d forgotten that his parents, especially his mother, seemed to have eyes in the back of their heads. Crestfallen at his stupidity, he silently sobbed. All he wanted to do was escape to his room, shut the door, curl up in a ball on his bed and hide from the world, but, right now, there was no escape. Instead, he stood stoically and waited for his mother to go mental. If only Amelia was here, she would stop Mum from fussing.

‘Well?’ Charlotte asked.

Looking down at his muddy, scuffed shoes, Dillan answered, ‘It was an accident. I was looking at my phone. I didn’t see the broken branch laying on the pavement and I tripped over it and fell.' He looked up at his mother. She had a strange expression on her face and he wondered what she was thinking. He just hoped she believed him because no way could he tell her what had really happened. There was no branch, it was the foot of Bradley Jenkins that had suddenly stuck out in front of him and the push from Connor Brooks that had him down on his knees, his phone slithering down the path.

'What is it with you boys that you must have your head in your phone all the time. Dillan what am I going to do with you?'

Dillan shrugged his shoulders. There was nothing anyone could do.

'Go on, get your muddy shoes off and your trousers and I'll sort them.'

'Mum! Not my trousers. I can do that in my room. I'm nearly a young man.'

The ringing of a phone had Charlotte spinning round and heading back to the kitchen. 'Just get your shoes off and when you've changed out of your uniform, bring the trousers to me,' she called over her shoulder as she hurried to answer her phone.

Not waiting for his mother to return, Dillan kicked off his shoes and in his stocking feet, he raced up the stairs.

Once inside his room, Dillan shut the door and leaning against it, he sank down onto his hunkers. Cradling his head in his folded arms, he let his tears escape and as they cascaded down his face, he sobbed, a heartrending sound. What a day it had been. He'd had two days of the silent treatment, which was just as much a worry and as frightened as he was, he'd kept a low profile, then today Bradley decided to talk to him. 'Come on mate, we're buddies, aren't we?' Bradley had draped his arm around his shoulders and winked at him. He wasn't fooled. They were supposed to be friends, at least he'd thought they were, but when Connor joined their class, things changed. Bradley looked up to Connor as if he was some kind of God and his friendship became malicious.

Wiping his eyes on the sleeve of his jacket. He stared ahead, his room was the only place he felt safe these days, but he had to go to school – or at least pretend he was going. He'd missed school on and off for a few weeks. Even this past week he'd not turned up for a couple of days, but after seeing one of his mother's friends, a neighbour, he had panicked and had reluctantly gone back to school. He was certain she hadn't seen him and more so because his mother had not mentioned it.

'Dillan, please bring down your muddy trousers,' Charlotte called up the stairs.

Startled at hearing his mother's voice, he pushed himself up, took off his jacket and threw it on the chair next to his desk. It missed the chair and landed on the floor. He shrugged at the crumbled heap then sank on the edge of his bed.

He pulled off his muddy trousers and was shocked at how filthy they were. He'd been more worried about his phone being broken that he'd not noticed how dirty and wet his clothes were. With his legs now exposed, several black and blue bruises, plus other nasty cuts and injuries were revealed. He gently rubbed at them. They were still sore from last week's kicking. At the memory, he felt fresh tears prick at his eyes. Connor and Bradley were sneaky: they never hurt him when anyone was able to see what they were doing. Instead, they made sure they were either alone, or they inflicted pain surreptitiously. The bruises on his legs were from one of those moments. Connor and Bradley had sat down at the same table as him in the library. The tables were big enough for up to eight students, but Connor made sure his books were spread out across the table so there was no room for anyone else. Seeing them arrive and sit down, he'd got up.

'Excuse me, Dillan, but I thought you said you would help me with my project,' Connor said in a voice loud enough to attract the teacher. Turning towards him the teacher had smiled. 'Good to hear you boys are helping each other. That's the spirit.' Dillan had sunk back down on his chair knowing there was no escape.

Connor sat down and kicked him on the shins.

'Thanks for your kind offer of help,' Connor scoffed as the teacher turned away.

He'd tried not to show how painful the kick had been as Bradley sat next to Connor. Bradley kept a sly look on the teacher and pretended to read and take notes and all the while they both swung their feet and kicked into his legs. He'd tucked his legs under his chair, but Connor laughed at him before dropping down under the table as if to retrieve his pen and then stabbed him twice with a compass point.

The sound of his mother's voice outside on the landing had Dillan jumping up. He grabbed a pair of jogging pants from the bottom of his wardrobe. He'd just managed to pull them on, enough to hide the mess of his legs, when his mother stormed in.

'If Mohammed won't come to the mountain, then the mountain must go to Mohammed,' Charlotte chanted as she placed a tray with a sandwich and drink on his bedside cabinet. 'This will keep you going until dinner.'

Dillan looked on bewildered before uttering a thank you.

Charlotte then picked up the crumpled trousers, draped them over her arm before striding across the room to where Dillan's jacket lay on the floor. She picked it up, shook it out and placed it around the back of his desk chair. She smirked and then threw him a *what is the matter with you* look but remained silent.

Dillan gave her a distant look, she could give him all the looks she liked, but she would never guess why he behaved like he did. Part of him was grateful despite needing help, but then how would she understand?

'Get your homework done and then we can eat,' she smiled as she spoke, then headed to the door. Hanging on to the handle, she turned and took in her son.

'Is everything OK Dillan?'

'Everything is fine. I'm just sorry, I tripped and made a mess of my trousers and my phone.' He was surprised how normal he sounded and how easy he lied these days.

Charlotte walked over and wrapped her arms around him 'I hope so, because you're my special boy.' She kissed the top of his damp head. Dillan's phoned pinged with more messages. 'Do your homework before you answer your messages.' Dropping another kiss on his blonde head, Charlotte left the room.

He watched as his mother walked out and he really wanted to call her back and talk to her, but how could he?

Chapter THREE – Dillan

That Saturday, his mother had taken him into the city to a shop that specialised in repairing mobile phone screens. Thankfully she'd not made any more fuss about what had happened. Afterwards, she had taken him to a one of his favourite places for a burger and chips. It took all his strength to eat it without throwing up. He had always devoured the food there, but these days he felt so on edge with everything and was afraid that Bradley and Connor might appear at any moment. Of course he should feel safe, but if they did turn up, he knew they would pretend to be all good friends and his mother would see that as great and likely invite them to have a burger. Even such an act of kindness would create more problems for him and make his life a hundred times worse. Needing to get back home as soon as possible, he scoffed down his burger and hoped it wouldn't want to return!

'I'm not sure whether to be pleased you enjoyed your burger or annoyed at your manners,' Charlotte said, watching her son demolish his food.

Dillan couldn't quite read Charlotte's expression and guessed it was the latter.

Several days had passed since the incident that had caused his phone screen to be smashed. Now he stood outside the very burger place he and his mum had visited after getting his phone screen repaired. Thankfully his screen was still intact. To ensure it stayed that way, he had spent the weekend hiding, but his phone had pinged as if messaging were going out of fashion. None needed a response; they were either sick emojis or words that called him names, unbelievable names. He'd deleted them all. He sighed at the nightmare of his life and checked his watch. He should be in school, but he knew he couldn't face another day there. On Monday, he'd told his mother he felt sick and had a problem with his tummy. It was the truth, though feeling sick was more about fear than a bug. The look on her face had told him she didn't believe him. He'd tried not to cry, but tears had slipped down his cheeks. To his surprise, she'd scooped him up in her arms and hugged him tight. He wanted to tell her what was happening but couldn't cope with the consequences if she kicked off with the school. And worse, who would believe him? Still hugging him, his mother had agreed he didn't have to go to school. He'd almost collapsed with relief. She had worked from home that day. On Tuesday, she had told him he needed to go to school. She couldn't be more wrong, but arguing with her wouldn't get him another day at home. He had no idea how he would cope and with his backpack slung over his shoulder, he'd set off down the path that ran between Carlton Road and Colville Way. It was a wide path with streetlights and was used by local residents especially pupils attending Thorpe Manor school which was located off of Colville Way. His plan was to get into class, keep his head down and do his schoolwork. For him, Tuesday was one of the better days for the teachers. Mrs Wilson and Mr Barraclough, both had total control of the class and a silent respect from all students. During these lessons he felt safe. Both teachers would walk between the desks keeping a close eye on everyone. It gave him a chance to try and do his lessons. Of course, Dillan would have preferred to stay at home again, but that wasn't an option. Lost in his thoughts as he made his way along the path, he hadn't heard the footsteps hurrying behind. A hand on his shoulder had brought him to an abrupt stop. Then Connor appeared at his side. His heart raced and his feeling of safety plummeted.

'Didn't see you at school yesterday. Been a poorly baby?' Connor taunted.

He'd decided not to answer and prayed that someone else would walk along the path.

'We should be friends. Bradley says you two used to be. So what happened?'

Dillan wished he had the courage to say, *you came along*, instead he'd shrugged his shoulders.

'Right from now on, we *are* friends, don't forget that and I'll be watching you. Let's shake on it.' Connor held out his hand.

He'd stood still and stared down at his feet. He knew Connor didn't mean a word of what he'd just said.

'Come on, let's shake on friendship.'

Knowing it wasn't the right thing to do, he'd reluctantly held out his hand.

Connor took hold and shook it, 'See we are friends now.'

Keen to get his hand out of Connor's grip, he'd pulled away, but Connor was quick and grabbed it. This time he'd twisted it and the pain had shot up his arm.

'Friends, right? Don't forget and if you do, I'll kill you.' Sniggering, Connor had eventually let go and slapped him across the head. An evil grin had filled his face. 'Now walk with me to school.'

Rubbing his arm, he'd kept pace with Connor, but avoided eye contact. He wasn't sure how much longer he could deal with this. Making himself invisible would be the answer or even dead. No one would care. Then he thought of his parents and sister, maybe they would miss him. As they'd approached the end of the path, Bradley stood waiting for them. He'd stared at Connor with a puzzled look on his face.

'What's going on here?' Bradley looked from Connor to Dillan and back to Connor.

'Young Dillan has just realised how great friends we all are.'

Dillan hadn't missed the look of amusement on Bradley's face. He too had insisted they were friends the other day and knew it was just another way of tormenting him. What to do about it? He had no idea.

Now as he stood looking through the burger restaurant's large windows, he couldn't believe how the morning that had held a modicum of promise had ended in disaster. Mrs Wilson along with two other members of staff were off sick. The teacher's rota had been moved around to such a point that Mr Barraclough didn't take their class. Instead, they had Miss Harvey, a supply teacher; a kind, jolly person, but she didn't have the command of the class like Mr Barraclough and Mrs Wilson. And to add the final nail in his coffin, Connor had moved to sit next to him and with no objection from Miss Harvey, he had enjoyed his covert bullying. Connor quickly swapped his exercise book with Dillan's and before Dillan could grab it back, Connor wrote a few words.

Miss Harvey had called out, but before Dillan could speak, she'd moved on to another member of the class. Then she marched back to look over at his book. She'd glared at him and then at Connor. 'See me after the lesson, Dillan,' she had commanded before marching away.

'Say thank you,' Connor had hissed, a malicious sneer on his face.

Dillan had stared at him and was surprised when he mouthed, 'For what?'

'For attracting the teacher to your command of English,' Connor smirked. And as he did so, Connor stabbed Dillan with what looked like a short knitting needle. Dillan choked down the need to scream, turning it into a loud cough instead. It had done nothing to attract help other than a dark look from Miss Harvey.

'Now we're friends I shall be sitting next to you from now on,' Connor said to Dillan. At the same time, Connor had pinched his thigh in the same place he had stabbed him moments earlier. By the end of the lesson, Dillan thought he would faint. As soon as the bell went, Miss Harvey had stood at the open classroom door and ushered everyone out.

'Not you Dillan. I need a word with you.' She had said in a stern voice indicating Dillan should go over to her desk. Connor, with Bradley in tow, had looked over his shoulder and sniggered.

Alone with Miss Harvey Dillan had feared the worst.

'Sit down, Dillan,' Miss Harvey had pointed to a chair next to her desk.

Dreading what was to come, Dillan had perched on the edge of the plastic chair.

'Now what is going on?' She had glared at him as she spoke.

‘Sorry, I don’t understand,’ he had said and tucked his hands under his legs to try and stop them from shaking.

‘Dillan, please look at me when you speak,’ she had commanded.

Cautiously, he’d looked up. It was only then that Miss Harvey continued. ‘I think you do. The class might think it runs rings around me, but rest assured, I am no fool. So, tell me Dillan, what really is going on?’ This time her voice had sounded softer.

‘Nothing Miss. If you are referring to Connor moving to sit next to me, it was his decision.’

‘What about yours?’

He had looked down at his knees.

'Dillan are you being bullied?’

How was he to answer that question, he had thought. If he said yes, all hell would break loose and he would be dealt with by Connor and Bradley. If he said no, then he would lose any chance of help. He couldn’t win whatever he was to answer. ‘No Miss I’m not.’

‘Really! In that case you can go, but I am here to listen and help if it turns out different.’

‘Thank you, Miss.’ He had almost ran out of the classroom so relieved to be able to get away.

Now as his mind went over what had happened that morning, he had so wanted to tell Miss Harvey everything, but he couldn’t. Instead, he had left school and walked into town. He knew he couldn't go back to school. He would take a few days off wandering around the streets and through the park whilst he worked out what he could do. It wasn't going to be easy. But he had to come up with something.

Chapter FOUR – Charlotte and Dillan

Dropping her car fob on the hall table, Charlotte kicked off her court shoes. Her feet ached, she hated wearing them, but she'd had back-to-back meetings with clients all day and felt she needed to dress appropriately and trainers on her feet were not appropriate! Once her meetings were over, she'd checked her phone and saw she had two new voice mails. The first message was from a neighbour talking about Dillan, the second was from school asking her to call them. She had listened to the neighbour's message with annoyance. The one from the school had been vague saying it was nothing to be alarmed about but had asked her to call them. She had tried to call back, but it had gone straight to voice mail. Her mind was going over what their neighbour, Lizzie Hughes, had said and could only assume that was why the school needed to talk to her. She tried a couple more times, but with her calls still going to voice mail, she decided to try again in the morning. Had it been urgent someone would have either answered her calls or phoned her back. Right now, she needed to ask Dillan a few questions. She sighed heavily; it had been a fraught day and the last thing she needed right now was more stress. Feeling the weight of the day both physically and mentally, she padded through to the kitchen and, as tired as she felt, she tried to work out what was the best way to deal with the situation. She had suspected something was not right for some time but had hoped she was overthinking it. As she switched on the coffee machine, she heard the front door open. Heading back into the hall, she was met by Dillan.

'Hello Dillan. Where have you been today?'

Closing the door, Dillan dropped his bag down on the hall floor and in a startled voice, he answered. 'School of course.'

'Really?'

With his hands stuffed in his pockets, he ignored his mother and headed towards the stairs.

'Dillan, I need to talk to you. Please come back.'

He stopped in his tracks but didn't turn round.

'Why have you been in the town this afternoon?'

Dillan swung round, wide-eyed and his face turning red.

'And before you tell me you've been at school all day, I know different. Mrs Hughes from down the road, phoned to tell me that she'd seen you and said it wasn't the first time. She was concerned.'

Pulling a face, he turned round as he thought quickly and said, 'If you don't believe me, you can ask Miss Harvey, she took our class this morning and she spoke to me after class.'

'Did she, now. I hope it was to praise your work.' Though Charlotte had her doubts, considering the call from the school. 'And what about this afternoon?' Though she had her reservation on that in light of the school phoning her.

'We were on a project and had to visit a few of the shops in town to get answers to questions.' As he responded, Charlotte's phone rang and she dashed off to answer it.

Dillan ran upstairs to his room. As he closed the door, he couldn't believe how quick he was at coming up with such a lie. He wished he was as clever with Connor and Bradley. Needing to check on his mother, he opened his bedroom door. He listened. Thankfully, she was still talking on the phone. Closing the door, he tried to keep the panic down as he quickly whipped off his trousers. The last thing he needed right now was his mother seeing his leg. Stepping into his house pants, he ran his fingers gently over his leg sores. He winced. They were killing him. Knowing he needed to keep calm, he pulled his pants up. And if the state of his leg wasn't bad enough, Miss Harvey had asked him to stay behind after class because of the filth Connor had written in his exercise book. Oddly enough, she had never mentioned it. Instead, Miss Harvey had seen something going on, enough for her to ask if he was being bullied. It had taken him aback because Connor was very sneaky and sly. How on earth could he tell her. She had no idea what they did to him and how they made him feel. She would never be able to save him from Connor and Bradley and even more now that Connor insisted they were friends. And who would believe a snivelling big sissy who couldn't stand up for himself. Connor and Bradley commanded respect and fear in equal measures. There was no way Connor would let him out of his sight. He'd watch him like a hawk, ready to pounce at any opportunity. What was he to do? And what could he do? The situation was impossible.

'Dillan,' his mother trilled, pushing open the door. Dillan almost fell off his bed at the surprise of her appearing. 'Dillan, are you alright?' As she spoke, she crossed over to the bed and sat next to him. Dillan hung his head and placed his hands on his knees. He needed to stop the tears that were pricking at his eyes.

'Dillan are you having trouble at school?' As Charlotte spoke, she wrapped her arms around him. 'Come give your mum a cuddle.' He didn't resist as she held him close to her. 'I know there is something not right. You've been so quiet of late. What is going on? Is someone bothering you?'

Twice in one day someone had asked him that question. Was it so obvious? He desperately wanted to talk to someone, but where to start and how to make it go away. Telling his mum would only make things much worse. He knew she would go to his school and that would cause so much trouble he would never be able to go there again and be safe. The truth is, he would never be safe again.

Unaware of Dillan's inner turmoil, Charlotte gently slackened her grip on her son and looked into his face. 'You know school phoned me today. I don't know what they want as I couldn't speak to anyone. Do you know what they might want to talk to me about?'

Dillan swallowed down a lump that threatened to choke him and despite all his efforts he felt the tears slip down his cheeks.

'Hey, whatever it is, it can't be that bad.' Charlotte tenderly wiped at his tears with her fingers. 'I'm sure it is something that can be sorted easily once I manage to talk to someone. Maybe, you would like to talk to me?'

Unable to speak, he nodded.

'Is it something at school?' as she spoke, she touched his leg. Dillan cried out. 'What have you done to your leg?' Before Dillan could move away, Charlotte took hold of his pants and gently rolled up the leg. 'Good God! What has happened here?' She stared down at livid sores and dark bruises.

'How did this happen?' she exclaimed in horror 'When did this happen? Who did this? We need to clean this up or it could go septic!' All the time she spoke, Dillan remained still and silent.

‘Leave your pants off until I’ve bathed these sores.’

Getting to her feet, Charlotte stood in front of her son waiting for an answer. As his silence continued, she hunkered down, and with both hands she cupped his face and looked into his sad eyes. ‘Please talk to me. Please tell me what is going on. I know something is very wrong, but I can’t help if you won’t talk to me. Please talk to me,’ she pleaded. ‘Please tell me what is going on.’

'It’s not easy to talk about.’

‘What is not easy to talk about? Dillan, are you being bullied at school?’

Dillan looked into his mother’s face. ‘It’s not that bad.’

Unable to keep the emotion out of her voice, she cradled Dillan in her arms. He was still her baby and at thirteen he should be happy and not deeply upset. ‘How long has this been going on?’ She released him as she spoke.

Dillan shrugged his shoulders. ‘It’s doesn’t matter. Not long.’

‘I want to believe you, but something tells me this has not happened overnight.’ Taking hold of his hands, ‘Is this how your phone screen was broken?’

Dillan nodded, but kept his eyes cast down.

Charlotte kissed the top of her son’s head as she stood up. Still holding his hands, in a gentle voice she spoke, 'For now, let's get those nasty marks on your leg sorted and then we can talk if you want to. I will be going to school tomorrow to talk to the teachers. I promise it will all be fine.' Charlotte wasn't sure what was worse - her anger at what was happening to her son or her guilt for not noticing something before now. Both vied for pole position.

'Please don't! It will make things worse and I can handle it. Please Mum!' Dillan was almost hysterical with fear at what his mother was planning to do.

'Dillan, calm down. It can't continue.'

Dillan stared at his mother in horror.

'You've nothing to worry about and you are staying home tomorrow until I have everything sorted. OK?'

Dillan didn't respond. His mind was already in panic overdrive at how things had escalated since he'd arrived home. What was he going to do?

'Come on, let's get your leg bathed.' As Charlotte spoke, she gently pulled Dillan up from the bed and led him downstairs to where the medical box was kept.

Chapter FIVE - Dillan

Dillan gazed out of the window and looked on as houses and busy roads melted away to open fields. He leaned back in his seat and for the first time in many months, felt he could breathe again. Even the constant tightness in his chest appeared to have eased. His eyes slowly closed. Realising he could easily fall asleep, he snapped them open. He must try and keep awake. Turning back to the window he told himself to concentrate on the passing scene to stop him from drifting off. He'd barely slept the previous night; his mind going over and over the only thing to do. He hated himself for not being able to deal with the situation, but he had to do something and despite his tiredness, he now had a plan. His mother had said he could stay home from school as she would be talking to the headmaster and teachers. But no matter what she had said he had no intentions of ever going back to school. His mother was not only going to *his* school, but by now would be talking to the teachers and headmaster. He silently groaned at what his mother was doing. Before she had left the house, she'd received a call from Miss Harvey. He had positioned himself on the stairs to listen to the conversation, but all he had heard was his mother saying, *'Really! Of course and yes, I will be there!'* She had ended the call adding that she was looking forward to talking to her and the headmaster. How bad could it get? He gave out an audible groan distracting the elderly man opposite who peered over his newspaper.

Keeping his gaze on the passing scenery his mind wandered back to the previous evening. His mother had tried to encourage him to talk to her about why he was upset and of course the livid marks on his leg. He was so exhausted and frightened that he'd admitted to being bullied. It was a mistake and he had quickly added that it was under control and nothing to worry about. Now everything would just explode and instead of helping, it would turn into the worse nightmare. How had it come to this? He ran his hands over his face as if by doing so it could help erase the last few months, and importantly, yesterday. Just thinking about his mother at his school had his heart beating faster than a drum roll. The tightness in his chest was back. Why did she have to get involved? As soon as he had watched her car pull out of the drive, he had collected his bag and headed straight to the railway station. It was late enough for everyone to be in school and the chances of meeting anyone who might know him or his family was zero. He had almost run in his haste to get away. Now all he could think of was where he was going. He'd turned his phone off; it would stop the onslaught of messages and also his mother trying to call him. He closed his eyes to try and forget everything for a moment.

'Hello, young man,' a voice called and at the same time a hand gently squeezed Dillan's shoulder. He woke with a start; the rhythm of the train had lulled him to sleep.' Sorry to wake you, but I need to see your ticket,' the conductor said in a polite and friendly voice.

With blurry eyes, Dillan stared up at the young lady who smiled down at him. 'Are you OK?' she asked.

He nodded. 'I'm fine,' he said rummaging into his jacket pocket for his ticket. 'Here it is,' and offered the ticket to the conductor.

Checking the ticket, she looked down at Dillan. 'Cambridge. Ten minutes and we'll be there, best you stay awake,' she continued to smile and handed back his ticket.

'Thank you,' he said and tucked the ticket back into his pocket. He watched as the conductor made her way through the carriage. He was shocked that he had fallen asleep. He didn't want to think what might have happened if the conductor hadn't come along. Keeping his gaze out of the window, he thought about the next stage of his journey.

As the train approached Cambridge station, Dillan checked the details on the palm of his hand. He'd written them there after checking Google maps as he'd no intentions of switching his phone back on. Thankfully, they were still legible.

Feeling nervous, he left the railway station and thought about the rest of his journey. Part of him wanted to hurry, yet another didn't want to. Everything seemed so complicated and his head ached like it was being assaulted with a heavy instrument. For a moment he thought he was going to throw up and stopped at the side of a waste bin. He waited for a few seconds before continuing.

Forty minutes later, having taken two wrong turnings, he sat on the wide paved step of a contemporary house designed for students. He had rung her bell, but there was no response. He wasn't expected but had hoped his sister would be home. How long it would be before she was, he had no idea and too afraid to switch on his phone, he would have to wait. Resting his head against the stone wall next to the front door, Dillan fell asleep.

Chapter SIX - Amelia

With her lecture over, Amelia made her way home. It had been a tough class and she would need to study hard over the weekend. It was mid-afternoon and she could cram in more studying if she put her mind to it. That evening, she had been invited out with friends, but night clubs were not her scene and had politely declined. Her studies were more important. She was in her second year and had worked hard to get a university place and even more when she had secured a place at Cambridge. The hardest thing had been leaving home and having to learn to do everything herself. Thankfully her parents and Dillan had visited often during her first year. Dillan, she knew missed her and she did her best to keep in touch through messages, though the last few months she had noticed he'd been unusually quiet - not his usual chatty self. She'd asked him if he was OK and he'd said he was, but she felt things were not quite as OK as he suggested. There had been a number of times when she had pushed him to talk, but he had always been adamant he was fine. She just hoped he was. Maybe it was his hormones kicking in. Hers played havoc with her moods, she thought. With one hand on her shoulder bag and the other in her pocket, Amelia picked up her pace as she headed back to her pretty, yet small, one-bedroomed apartment. With each step her mind drifted back to her latest assignment. She was struggling with it and knew she needed to give as much attention as possible to gain the best marks. She felt honoured to be studying at Cambridge, though far too often felt she was out of her depth. Lost in her thoughts, her head down and on auto pilot, she turned onto the path that led to the short flight of steps and the front door of Victor House. Pulling out her key, Amelia looked up and came to a sudden halt.

'Dillan!' she cried. 'What are you doing here?'

Dillan jumped to his feet and stared at his sister.

Amelia raced up the steps and stood in front of Dillan. 'Does mum know you are here?' Even as she asked the question, she knew the answer.

She quickly unlocked the door and taking hold of Dillan's arm, she pulled him inside.

'Come on,' she said as she led him further in to the apartment. Her mind racing. What had happened that had Dillan parked on her doorstep?

After taking their coats off. She sat Dillan down on the two-seater sofa while she perched herself on the edge of the low table, facing him. She looked into his face. What she saw was a picture of misery. All thoughts of her assignment were gone; her mind raced on what was happening and why Dillan was here and wondered where to begin.

'Dillan, what is going on? How did you get here?'

As if unable to speak, Dillan looked down and picked at his fingers.

'I'm going to phone Mum. No doubt she thinks you are at school.'

Dillan shook his head.

'If not at school, where does she think you are?' Her voice was an octave higher than normal as she tried to process what was going on. She reached for her bag and pulled out her phone. All the while questions filled her head as to what had caused Dillan to run to her. Having pushed the button for her mum, she listened to ringing tone.

Dillan remained silent.

'Mum,' Amelia cried at the sound of her mother's voice. 'I have Dillan here with me. Please tell me what is going on?' Amelia listened and could hear the panic in her mother's voice. 'He's fine, yes. No, I don't know anything at the moment. Yes, of course, but I have just arrived home and found him sitting on the doorstep. OK. I will do my best.' The call ended.

Amelia placed her phone next to her on the low table. Looking at Dillan she could see a mixture of emotions crossing his face. 'Mum is on her way. Dillan you must talk to me. Poor Mum is beside herself. She went to your school today, did you know?'

Dillan nodded.

'Do you want to talk about today or what is happening to you? Dillan, please look at me.'

To Amelia's surprise, Dillan moved forward, dropped down on his knees and threw his arms around her. Instantly, she wrapped her arms around her little brother and hugged him tight. For several moments he clung to her, her heart breaking as he sobbed, his tears soaking into her top.

'Come on, Dillan, please tell me what is making you so unhappy,' she soothed and with her left hand stroked his hair. Gently, she moved him back onto the sofa and sat next to him. Spying a box of tissues on the side table, she reached over and pulled them towards her. Grabbing a handful out, she handed them to Dillan. Keeping a couple she wiped at his face. She wanted to cry at the utter misery she saw, but swallowed down her emotions for now.

'Dillan.'

With a tear-stained face and red eyes, Dillan stared at his sister. 'I can't do it anymore. I just want it to stop and to die,' his words came out slowly interspersed with sobs.

'What can't you do anymore?'

Dillan looked down at his hands.

'Does Mum know why you are so unhappy?'

He shook his head. 'Not really, though I did mention something last night. I know she went to school today.' Fresh tears sprung from his eyes.

'What did you tell her?'

'If only you were at home, you would have been there to talk to and I'm sure it would all be fine by now.' Dillan took hold of Amelia's hand.

She squeezed it gently. 'Tell me what's been happening. I'm here now to listen and help.'

With his eyes cast down, he pulled his hand away and locked them together on his knee. 'They don't stop. If they are not hurting me, then they send messages day and night.'

'Who does?'

'Connor and Bradley.'

'I thought Bradley was your friend?'

'He was and when Connor came to our school they became friends. Connor is mean and Bradley is afraid of him and so does what he wants.'

'And bullying you, is what they do?'

Dillan nodded.

'Can you tell me what they have done to you?'

'Everything. They broke my phone screen twice. They kick, punch and spit at me. Make sure I am the one who gets caught if there is a teacher around. They've stabbed me.' He looked over at his sister. 'It doesn't sound all that bad now I say it.'

'Well, that sounds very bad to me.'

'It's not always what they do to me, it's the fact it never stops.'

'Why haven't you spoken to someone about this?'

Dillan gave out a snort. 'You don't understand. They would kill me.' Dillan glared at Amelia. 'They've told me a few times that they were plotting to do away with me. I can't ever go back and they must never know I've spoken to you about it all. You've no idea what they are like.'

Nothing had prepared Amelia for such a horrific outpouring. It was harrowing. As angry as she was, she knew she must remain calm. 'You said they message you. Have you still some of the messages?'

'No.'

Amelia thought carefully about her next question. 'Dillan is your phone switched off. I ask because Mum said she's been ringing you and you don't answer?'

He nodded.

'Is it because of the messages?'

'Please don't tell Mum about any of this, please!'

'I think she is going to know when she arrives and you will have to talk to her.'

'I can tell you, there is nothing anyone can do.'

'Can I look at your phone?'

Dillan appeared to think about it, then slipped his hand into his pocket and pulled out his phone. He gave Amelia his passcode.

Once switched on and the passcode entered, Amelia was shocked to see over forty messages unread. There was several from Mum, but the rest were from either Connor or Bradley. She skimmed through them; they were vile. For each one she did a screen shot and sent them to her phone. It took time but needed doing.

'What are you doing?' Dillan asked, his voice rising in panic.

'Just in case these get deleted, I have taken copies.'

Dillan looked on in horror. 'I have never kept the messages.'

Amelia leaned over and squeezed his hand. 'Trust me Dillan. We need these.'

As if the very life had drained out of him, he sat and stared at the phone in Amelia's hand.

Once again tears trickled down his cheek. He wiped the back of his hand across his face. 'They'll kill me if you or Mum show those to anyone. I can't do it anymore and I can't go back to school. I'm not like them, I don't like being mean to others. I did stand up to them at first, but it made it so much worse.' He looked into Amelia's face. 'Please, don't tell anyone. Please!'

The anger in her was immeasurable, but between her and her parents, they would sort this. Never could she believe this sort of thing could happen to anyone let alone her little brother. Swallowing her anger, she gave Dillan a reassuring hug. 'Let me make us a cup of tea and you a sandwich. Would you like that?'

Dillan nodded.

Amelia rose and walked over to the tiny kitchen area. She checked her watch and knew it would be some time before her mum arrived. In the meantime, she needed to try and find a way to calm Dillan and reassure him all will be fine.

Holding a tray with a mug of tea and a cheese sandwich, Amelia moved back to where Dillan had slumped on the sofa. She looked down at her brother and saw he was fast asleep. Placing the tray on the low table, she went into the bedroom and brought out the duvet from her bed. Resting his head on a cushion, she placed the duvet over him. For the first time since he had arrived, he looked peaceful. Gazing down at him, her emotions took free reign and unchecked tears cascaded down her cheeks. He was her baby brother, she loved him so much and no one was going to hurt him again.

Chapter SEVEN – Charlotte

Charlotte could not believe how anyone travelled anywhere these days. The traffic was almost at a standstill. The A11 was a nightmare at best, but today it seemed at its worst. Staring at a sea of red taillights, she thought about the events of the last few hours. Her mind was in turmoil. What had she missed? What had she not noticed and what had she not heard? She was mother to two beautiful children and loved them more than anything else in the world. They were good parents. At least they had always believed that to be, but if that was so, why hadn't she noticed Dillan was changing? Had she put it down to his age? Had she been too busy to listen to him? Surely not! Steve, could be a little tough at times, telling Dillan to man up! But there was no question that he loved both his children and only ever wanted the best for them. Despite the huge time difference she had phoned him last night and told him about Dillan's revelations on being bullied, describing the terrible sores and bruises on his leg. Finally, she had added that she had an appointment with the school. He had offered to catch the next plane home, but she had persuaded him to stay where he was. She needed to get to the bottom of what was going on and then maybe he could consider coming back if necessary. She knew it wasn't easy for him; the project he worked on was in the Far East and demanded almost all of his time. He was scheduled to be out there for three months and had only been gone a month. It was tough not always having him around, but over the years they had learnt to live with it. She had promised to let him know how she had got on at school. Though nothing had prepared her to be driving to Cambridge.

The radio twittered on about health statistics and other events that were out of her control. Not wanting to listen to such negativeness, Charlotte turned off her radio. Sha had her own stressful situation to deal with. Looking ahead and trying not to scream, *get a move on*, she strummed her thumbs on the leather steering wheel as an outlet to her frustration. Her day had gone from bad to disaster. Trying to call Dillan to no avail and then only to learn from Amelia that she had found him sitting on her doorstep. How on earth had he got himself there? She had asked herself enough times for it to be a mantra! So far, her day had been filled with annoyance and anxiety. Her visit to Dillan's school wasn't what she had expected. Just thinking about it, had her stress level shoot up to maximum.

After a formal greeting from the headmaster, she had been invited to sit down on a modern white plastic chair. Graham Peel, seated himself opposite at a modern white framed, glass top desk where he had steepled his fingers.

'Thank you for coming to the school, Mrs Mortimer. It is important when we have issues that we have a face to face with the parents. It makes it easier to sort them out. I'm sure you agree.'

Charlotte wasn't sure what she was supposed to agree with, but in her mind, it was far more than an issue. 'An issue, you say. I think it is much more than that?'

Graham Peel knitted his eyebrows together and lowered his hands to the desktop. 'Not attending school *is an* issue, but it is solvable and once we have the parents onboard, it is often resolved in an instant.'

Charlotte had known Dillan had missed school a couple of times of late, she had learnt this from Lizzie Hughes after she had seen Dillan in the town. His answer was that he'd been there on a school project, but that wasn't why she was here. 'I think we are at cross purposes; Dillan hasn't missed school and the occasions he's been away from the classroom is down to his projects.'

'Mrs Mortimer,' he gave her what he probably thought was his best headmaster smile that said, you have been taken for a fool. 'I am disappointed to have had to ask you here, but Dillan's absences have become a serious issue.'

'I am of the understanding that we are having this meeting because, my son, Dillan is being bullied.'

The look on the headmaster's face was a mixture of amusement and horror.

'I'm sure when Miss Harvey joins us, she will confirm this,' she added.

'Oh dear, I think we most certainly do have a misunderstanding, Mrs Mortimer. Firstly, Miss Harvey is in class and cannot be disturbed. She is a supply teacher.' He smiled at her as he spoke the words, *supply teacher*. His countenance indicated she should understand the position. She didn't. All she could think of was, what had Miss Harvey being a supply teacher to do with not speaking to her about Dillan? She had kept her comment to herself as she needed to impress about Dillan's bullying.

'Mr Peel, I am here at Miss Harvey's and your request and I want to get to the bottom of what is happening that has left my son traumatised and afraid to come to school.'

Graham Peel sat up right in his modern leather, swivel chair, his gaze squarely on Charlotte. 'Bullying is a serious accusation. The implications are far reaching not only for the victim, but the perpetrators. We have in place protocols for dealing with this should it be found to be happening in our school.' His gaze remained on Charlotte as if to imply she should tread carefully.

Charlotte considered Peel's words. 'I have not taken this lightly. My son told me he was being bullied and was afraid. I saw the mess on his leg last night that the bullies had inflicted on him.' All she could see in her mind's eye was her upset son with serious injuries. The images made her blood boil yet even as she spoke, Charlotte realised she was talking to a sceptic. She should have taken photos of those terrible stab wounds and bruises. There was still time.

'I don't disbelieve you, Mrs Mortimer, however, before anything can be considered we need evidence. By chance do we have a name or names?'

Charlotte shook her head. 'No.'

'Indeed. Then how am I or the school able to deal with this if we have no names? Maybe you have evidence, such as messages, social media posts anything that we can look at or perhaps a photo of the injuries you have mentioned?'

To Charlotte's dismay, she answered, 'No.' But she was not defeated by this headmaster's list of questions for proof. As much as she wanted to snap back, she kept her voice calm. 'I might not have all you have asked for, but I can easily produce a very frightened young boy. A young boy who is terrified of coming to school, hence why he's not been attending as you have mentioned. To me that is evidence enough to deal with this.'

'I understand and I will keep a close eye out, but I have to say, I have not witnessed anything untoward when I walk through the corridors and enter classrooms.'

Pushing back her chair, Charlotte rose. 'I want something done about my visit today and I will not rest until I hear something has been done.'

On his feet, Graham Peel walked around his desk and stood next to Charlotte. He placed a reassuring hand on her shoulder. 'Tell Dillan to come and see me tomorrow and we can have a chat. I am sure once we do so, we can sort this out. In the meantime, I will, as I said, keep an eye open, but I need names and evidence.'

'Rest assured, Mr Peel, evidence will be brought to your attention and then I want this dealt with.' She turned on her heals and marched out of the headmaster's office.

Charlotte had left the school totally deflated and very angry. She needed Dillan to talk to her and explain exactly what was going on. His melt down last night, she knew, was the tip of the iceberg and she was going to get to the bottom of it.

Now as she parked outside Victor House, Charlotte felt her stress level at an all-time high. Picking up her phone, she messaged Amelia to say she was outside and would she come down to talk to her.

Chapter EIGHT – Charlotte

Charlotte watched as Amelia ran down the short flight of steps and open the passenger door. 'Mum, why aren't you coming in?'

'I will, but I wanted to talk to you alone. How is Dillan?' Charlotte didn't miss the red eyes of her daughter that told her she had been weeping.

Settling into the passenger seat, Amelia answered the question. 'He's asleep now.' She looked at her mother and bit at her bottom lip. 'He's told me so much, it's heartbreaking. I can't believe he kept it all to himself.' Her lip quivered as she spoke.

Charlotte took hold of her daughter's hand and holding it to her lips, kissed it. 'I hope he will talk to me too, but we will get through this. I promise.'

Amelia nodded.

'I've been to the school today. There were more interested in Dillan not attending. When I brought up the subject of bullying, I was hit with the need for proof, names and school protocol. Protocol! What has that to do with it all? I have my son almost broken because of what has been going on and now I must provide proof! Did he show his leg to you?'

Amelia shook her head. 'No, but he talked about what has been happening to him. To my surprise and relief, he allowed me to look at his phone.' She took a breath and continued to bite at her bottom lip. 'The messages are vile. It is hard to comprehend that someone, whatever age, could send such things. I have taken the precaution of making screen shots as a backup.' She gazed at her mother, 'There is plenty of evidence there.'

Charlotte squeezed her daughter's hand. 'Thank you.' At this moment she felt as if her heart was about to shatter into tiny pieces. If only she had questioned more when he was moody and nonresponsive, but at thirteen she assumed it was his age, hormones slowly awakening. How could she have been so naive? Turning her thoughts back to what her daughter had done, Charlotte felt a ripple of pride and relief. Now there's evidence! 'Thank you for doing that - quick thinking on your part. We are going to need everything we can gather. I will not rest until something is done about this.' She smiled at Amelia, but even she knew it wouldn't reach her eyes. 'Come on let's go and see if Dillan has woken up.'

Arm in arm, mother and daughter headed back up the flight of steps and into Amelia's apartment.

'He's exhausted,' Charlotte said in a hushed tone as she seated herself on the edge of the low table.

She wanted so much to scoop him up, take him in her arms and never let him go.

'I'll make us a cup of tea,' Amelia suggested. 'Then I'll tell you all he's told me. ' Charlotte, mouthed, *thank you* and was aware, Amelia was struggling with this awful situation.

Charlotte could not take her eyes off her sleeping son. She didn't want to weep, but nothing could stop the dam that had built up and with a blink the dam broke and tears cascaded down her face.

It was an hour later before Dillan slowly opened his eyes. He looked from his mother to Amelia and gave a weak smile. 'Mum, I'm sorry.'

It took all her strength not to hug him, but Charlotte just stared at him with a broad smile. 'There is nothing to be sorry about. We just wish you had talked to us sooner.'

Pushing the duvet back, Dillan sat up. He looked to his sister. 'Have you told Mum?'

Amelia nodded.

Dillan looked at his mother.

'Dillan you have nothing to be sorry about and we will sort it.'

'You went to school today?'

'You know I did. The school needs evidence and names so that they can help. I believe you've told Amelia.'

Dillan nodded. 'I can't go back there, ever. It will be too dangerous for me.' Fresh tears sprang in Dillan's eyes.

Instantly, Charlotte took hold of her son and hugged him tight. 'You are not going back. We will sort a new school for you. You are safe. Now we know what has been going on, we can deal with it.' As Charlotte spoke, she had no idea how it would all be dealt with, but she would move heaven and earth to make sure her son would never be afraid to go out or to school again.

'Can I stay here, please?'

Releasing her hold on Dillan, Charlotte, spoke. 'No, you need to come home. Amelia's apartment is very small and she needs to study.'

With beseeching eyes, he stared from his mother to Amelia, 'Please!'

'If you are happy to sleep on the sofa, you can stay for a couple of days,' Amelia conceded. 'It will give us both time to catch up.'

As if someone had switched a light on, Dillan's face lit up. 'Thank you, I promise not to be any trouble.'

Charlotte looked at Amelia. 'Are you sure?'

'Yes. It will be good for both of us and you too. He will be fine and I will bring him home on the train.'

'If you are staying then I need to ask you to do something for me. Please would you write down everything that has happened to you over the last few months. Include the names too. We need this information to stop this happening to someone else.' She didn't add that the boys who had caused all this pain needed dealing with.

Dillan cast his eyes down. 'I've told Amelia everything including the names.'

'I understand and maybe Amelia will help you put it all down.' As she spoke, she turned to Amelia, who nodded.

'Is that a deal?'

Reluctantly, Dillan nodded.

'In that case, if you are going to be OK, I will head back and hope the traffic is better than when I came. Be a good boy and I'll call you when I get home.' She kissed the top of Dillan's head. 'I love you so much.'

'I love you too, Mum.'

'By the way, I've spoken to your dad.'

Dillan's face turned from a smile to worry.

'He's so very upset and was keen to fly home. I have said I will give him an update. He sends his love and told you not to worry.'

'Tell him I love him too.'

Chapter NINE – Dillan

He had been so happy that he had been able to stay with Amelia. As it turned out, he'd been allowed to stay for four days. His mum had left money so that he and Amelia could go and buy a few things he would need to get through. It had been fun shopping with his sister and drinking hot chocolate in many of the trendy cafés. For the first time in months, he'd felt happy and safe. Now as he emptied his bag out onto his bed, the old fears rushed back and the feeling of being normal these last few days began to melt away.

The doorbell rang out and he held his breath and waited. His fears rushing in and his hands started to shake.

A knock on his bedroom door startled him further. He had no idea who the visitor might be, but his mind raced to someone from school or worse - Bradley and Connor. He tried not to panic as he watched his door slowly open.

'Dillan there is someone who would like to talk to you.'

Dillan froze.

Not missing the look of fear on her son's face, Charlotte, wrapped a reassuring arm around his shoulder and added. 'There's nothing to worry about.'

He wasn't sure if he should laugh or cry at his fears. He was supposed to feel safe at home. This was not a good omen.

'Come on. They are waiting to talk to you,' Charlotte encouraged, smiling.

Shrugging off his mother's arm, reluctantly Dillan followed. He tried to peer around her to make sure there was no one else; the hall was empty.

Standing at the bottom of the stairs, his mother continued to encourage. 'Come on, she's in the kitchen.'

She! Who was she?

Having no choice, he followed his mother into the kitchen and there sitting at the island was Mrs Hughes cradling a mug of coffee.

'Hello Dillan.' Lizzie Hughes smiled at him as he entered.

'I've put you a glass of juice over there, so sit yourself down,' Charlotte said, pointing to a stool opposite Lizzie.

Dillan's mind raced, he couldn't work out why Mrs Hughes would want to be having coffee with his mother and asking to talk to him. 'Hello, Mrs Hughes,' he finally said.

'While you were at Amelia's, Mrs Hughes came to see me. She'd heard about what has been happening to you and was very concerned.'

Dillan shot Mrs Hughes a guarded look.

'I'm on your side, Dillan,' Lizzie reassured. 'I know quite a bit about what you have been through.'

Dillan could never imagine someone who was dressed immaculately, drove a smart car and was never seen without her lipstick on, could have any idea about what he'd been through.

'You see, I work for an organisation that helps young people who have been the victims of dreadful bullying.'

Dillan looked at his mother.

'I was aware Mrs Hughes worked for a charity, but I had no idea which one. It's a local one and she has been talking to me about what they do.'

'In your absence, your mother has been to our premises and spoken with Matt, the manager there and he has been told all about you. He would very much like to meet you.'

'I don't understand.' He looked down at his glass of juice.

'Dillan, it's a special school that helps young people like you go back to school.'

Staring at his mother, his face a picture of fear, he spoke. 'I can't. I don't think I could go back to school ever again.' Dillan's eyes filled with tears.

'There is nothing to be afraid of. Your mother and I will be with you. You can meet the teachers and the students, who too have been bullied. You can then see if it is for you. What do you say to that?'

Unsure about what he had heard from Mrs Hughes, he turned to his mother, 'What do you think, Mum?'

'I think we should at least go along. What have we got to lose?'

Three weeks had passed since Mrs Hughes had sat in their kitchen and spoken to him and his mother and for the first time in months, Dillan arrived home, his bag bulging with books and sports gear; he was smiling.

'How was school today?' Charlotte asked.

Dillan dropped his bag on the floor and with hurried steps went to his mother. He wrapped his arms around her. 'The best, thank you so much. I love you.' He knew as he felt the warmth from his mother it would be a long time, if ever, he would feel safe again or free from fear. Trusting people would always be difficult, but as long as he could stay at this special school, he just might be able to grow up and be a little near to normal. He wouldn't hold his breath, but he would try.

Charlotte hugged her son. 'I love you so much. You will never know just how much.' She let her tears fall; they were tears of joy and optimism. There was still a long road ahead, but they would get there. They were a close-knit family, they had

Lizzie Hughes and a very special school to help. And whatever happened in the future, she would keep a very close eye on her precious son no matter how old he was.

THE END

Printed in Great Britain
by Amazon

40679729R00037